CONNIE WILLIS

I Met a

Traveller

in an

Antique

Land

Connie Willis

SUBTERRANEAN PRESS 2018

THE terrible thing about Manhattan is that all the streets look alike. And I can hear New Yorkers screaming bloody murder already, asking indignantly, "How can you say that? The Village and the Upper West Side look *nothing* alike, and how could you possibly confuse Soho with Midtown?" and bleating about Carnegie Hall and Penn Station and the Met, but that's not what I'm talking about. I'm talking about the *streets*. Especially the cross streets, though what I'm talking about applies to long stretches of Broadway and the Avenues, too.

They've all got two or three restaurants and a deli, a hole-in-the-wall shop selling electronics and another one selling Yankees baseball caps and Statue of Liberty pencil sharpeners and Radio City Music Hall magnets. There's a Duane Reade and a newsstand and a branch bank or a fancy-dancy pet store or a shoe repair. And there are always hoardings, so that you have to walk half the block between plywood plastered with ads for Metallica or *Hamilton* or the Sells-Floto Circus. And maybe if you're a local, you can tell the difference between Petronelli's and Antonelli's and Antonio's Pizzeria, but to an out-of-towner like me, they all look as much alike as the Starbucks on every corner.

Which means even if you do happen on that great little antique store or bakery, you have no idea where it was and no way to find it again, unless it happened to be next door to Radio City Music Hall. Which it wasn't. Or unless you noted the cross streets. Which I didn't.

I was in New York doing publicity for my blog, Gone for Good, and meeting with editors about publishing it as a book when I found the bookstore.

I'd just finished doing an interview on Backtalk on WMNH, and Brooke had called to tell me the editor at Random House I was supposed to meet with cancelled our one-thirty appointment.

"Probably because he heard that train wreck of an interview and doesn't want Random House's name connected with a book-hater," I said, going outside. "Why the hell didn't you warn me I was walking into a set-up, Brooke? You're my agent. You're supposed to protect me from stuff like that."

"I didn't *know* it was a set-up, I swear, Jim," she said. "When he booked you, he told me he loved your blog, and that he felt exactly like you do, that being nostalgic for things that have disappeared is ridiculous, and that we're better off without things like payphones and VHS tapes."

"But not books, apparently," I said. The host hadn't even let me get the name of my website out before he'd started in on how terrible e-books and Amazon were and how they were destroying the independent bookstore.

"Do you *know* how many bookstores have gone under the last five years in Manhattan?" he'd demanded.

Yeah, and most of them deserved to, I thought.

I hadn't said that. I'd said, "Things closing and dying out and disappearing are part of the natural order. There's no need to mourn them."

"No need to *mourn* them? So it's fine with you if a legendary bookstore like the Strand, or Elliott's, shuts its doors? I suppose it's fine with you if books die out, too."

"They're not dying out," I said, "but if they were, yes, because it would mean that society didn't need them any more, just like it stopped needing buggy whips and elevator operators, so it shed them, just like a snake sheds its skin."

He snorted in derision. "That's the stupidest thing I've ever heard. Necessary things disappear every day. And what about all the things we don't realize are necessary till they're already gone?"

"Then society brings them back. Like LPs. And fountain pens."

"And what if we *can't* bring the thing back? What if it's too late, and it's already gone?"

Like the chance to have a decent interview, you mean? I thought. "That isn't how it works," I said, trying to keep my temper. "Bookstores aren't disappearing, they're just changing form. And so are books," and tried to explain about e-books and print-on-demand and libraries going digital.

"Digital!" he said. "How do you know all these digitized books won't be accidentally deleted. Or disappear into the ether, never to be seen again?"

"That's what the Cloud's for," I said. "It can store every book ever—"

He snorted again. "You've obviously never heard of Wheeler Field."

Wheeler Field? What the hell was Wheeler Field?

"Wheeler Field was an Army airfield in Hawaii during World War II," he said. "They got worried about sabotage, so they parked all the planes in the middle of the field. And when Pearl Harbor came along, one Japanese bomb took out the whole thing, bam! just like that. And according to your reasoning, that was proof we didn't need those airplanes."

"That isn't what—"

"And I suppose you don't think we need forests either. Or polar bears. I suppose you think closing one of the best bookstores in New York City is just fine?"

"Yes," I said. "If it had outlived its usefulness," and things really went downhill from there. By the time the hour was up, he'd accused me of everything from promoting illiteracy to setting fire to the Library at Alexandria.

"It wasn't that bad," Brooke said. "I thought you made some good points about how there are some books we'd be better off without, like *Fifty Shades of Grey* and *Meditate Your Way to a Wealthier You*. I loved that!"

"If I was so great, then why did Random House cancel the appointment?" I asked.

"Because he's leaving for a big meeting in London. There's supposed to be a big storm coming in tonight, and he moved his flight up a day to beat it."

Which was probably just an excuse. The sky, or at any rate the slice of it I could see between buildings, was devoid of clouds.

"He'll be back Friday," Brooke said, "and he wants to see you then."

"Okay," I said grudgingly. "But don't send him the podcast of that interview."

"I won't. Oh, by the way, HarperCollins said they'd like to meet you for drinks before your dinner meeting with Tor. Will that work? Five-thirty at Fiada's?"

"Yes," I said.

"Great. And till then, kick back. Or go see the city—the Statue of Liberty or the Empire State Building or something."

That wasn't a bad idea. Not the Empire State Building part—I had no desire to spend the afternoon standing in line with a bunch of idiot tourists—but I hadn't seen anything of Manhattan except what had been visible through the window of a taxi.

Now, with my Random House appointment cancelled, I'd have time to walk back uptown to my hotel and see some of the city along the way. It wasn't particularly cold for November, and, according to the map on my phone, it wasn't that far.

Wrong. The blocks between the avenues are three times as long as the ones between streets, and it was getting steadily colder. The sky had turned a leaden gray, and the wind whipping through the skyscraper canyons was really nasty. I decided to get a taxi and go back to my hotel after all, but they'd all unaccountably disappeared, and before I'd gone another block, it began to rain. And not an ignorable sprinkle—the cold, coat-soaking kind.

I spotted a guy one corner down selling umbrellas and ran over to buy one, but he was out by the time I got there. I had to walk forever before I found a newsstand that had some, and then wrestled for several blocks to get the damned thing up and then to keep the wind from turning it inside out, the net result being that I have no idea what street I was on. It might have been Thirty-sixth or Fifty-second, somewhere between Broadway and Madison Avenue. Or not.

At any rate, I was messing with the damned umbrella when the rain turned into a downpour, and I ducked into a recessed doorway and saw it was the entrance to a bookstore.

The old-fashioned kind of bookstore, about a foot and a half wide, with dusty copies of some leather-bound tome in the front window, and "Ozymandias Books" lettered in gilded copperplate on the glass.

These tiny hole-in-the-wall bookstores are a nearly extinct breed these days, what with the depredations of Barnes and Noble, Amazon, and Kindle, and this one looked like the guy on WMNH would be ranting about *its* closing on his next program. The dust on the display of books in the window was at least half an inch thick, and from the tarnished-looking brass doorknob and the pile of last fall's leaves against the door, it didn't look like anybody'd been in the place for months. But any port in a storm. And this might be my last chance to visit a bookstore like this.

The inside was exactly what you'd expect: an old-fashioned wooden desk and behind it, ceiling-high shelves crammed with books stretching back into the dimness. The store was only wide enough for a bookcase along each wall, one in the middle, and a space between just wide enough for a single customer to stand. If there'd been any customers. Which there weren't. The only thing in the place besides the guy sitting hunched over the desk—presumably the owner—was a gray tiger cat curled up in one corner of it.

The rest of the desk was piled high with books, and the stooped guy seated at it had gray hair and spectacles and wore a ratty cardigan sweater and a 1940's tie. All he needed was one of those green eye-shades to be something straight out of *84 Charing Cross Road*.

He was busily writing in a ledger when I came in, and I wondered if he'd even look up, but he did, adjusting his spectacles on his nose. "May I help you, sir?" he said.

"You deal in rare books?" I asked.

"Rarer than rare."

Which meant wildly expensive, but a glance outside showed me the rain was coming down in sheets, and it was still two and a half hours to my dinner appointment. And it wasn't as if I had to actually buy anything. If he'd let me browse, which if the books were that expensive, he probably wouldn't.

"Were you looking for anything in particular, sir?" he asked.

"No" was obviously the wrong answer, but if I named some title, it would be just my luck that they'd have it, and I'd be stuck paying two hundred bucks

for some tattered, mildewed copy. "I just thought I'd
look around," I said.

"Be my guest." He waved a hand at the shelves.
"We've got an enormous selection, I'm afraid."

Yeah, I thought, looking at the titles on the near-
est shelf. *And if it wasn't all stuff like* Surviving the
Y2K Apocalypse *and Gibbon's* History of the Liberty
of the Swiss *and* The Vagabond Boys Go to Bryce
Canyon, *you might actually be able to move some of
this merchandise.* "Thank you," I said, and he nodded and went back to writing in the ledger.

I started back along the narrow aisle, looking at
the books. Rare? Obscure was more like it. I didn't
recognize a single title in the whole first section and
only a couple of authors. Most of the names—Richard
Washburn Child, Ethel M. Dell, George Ade—I'd
never heard of. The books didn't seem to be arranged
in any particular order. A dark-red Moroccan-
leather-bound copy of *Nothing Lasts Forever: A Tale
of Pompeii* stood next to a torn paperback of *The
Watts Riots: What's Next?*, a 1950s anthropology
textbook, a dozen Harlequin romances, and a fancy
illustrated copy of *Fairy Tales for Wee Tots.*

Obviously not grouped by topic or by author. By
title? No, *Promise Me Yesterday* was cheek by jowl
with *A Traveller's Guide to Salisbury Cathedral,*
Herman Melville's *The Isle of the Cross*, and a 1928
Brooklyn phone book.

By price? I pulled out the Melville, but there was no slip in it and no price penciled lightly at the top of the first page, and nothing inside either *Promise Me Yesterday* or the Salisbury cathedral guide. Which must mean *really* expensive, though I refused to believe it or the phone book was worth more than a couple of dollars, to say nothing of Finlay's *Common Diseases of Holstein Cattle*. And *The Dionne Quintuplets in Hollywood.*

Maybe the owner was an eccentric who was actually only interested in collecting books, not selling them, but the shelves were too neatly arranged, and as I worked my way toward the back, the books became less dust-covered and somehow newer looking, though the titles didn't bear that out. Here was *Ocean to Cynthia* by Sir Walter Raleigh and Ben Jonson's *Richard Crookback.*

There still didn't seem to be any rhyme or reason to the books' arrangement. There was a *Nine Steps to No-Effort Weight Loss* on the same shelf as the Raleigh, and *The Corpse in the Larder* stood next to *Grace Holmes' Junior Year at Rosetree College.* And a *Tiger Beat* picture bio of Leonardo DiCaprio, circa the movie *Titanic* and cashing in on his then heartthrob status.

That could not possibly be considered a rare book by any definition, and I was about to take it up to the front and ask the guy at the desk how much they wanted for it when a beautiful blonde in a black pencil skirt and high heels brushed past me, heading for the front. I was suddenly really glad I'd come into Ozymandias's.

"Has Jude come in yet?" the blonde asked the guy at the desk, which meant she must work here, though she didn't look the part. She looked like she should work at Bloomingdale's. Or *Vogue*. And Ozymandias's didn't look like it could afford any staff at all, let alone three people.

"Have you heard from her, Arthur?" she asked. "We're swamped back there."

Back *where?* I couldn't see anybody else at the back of the store. And come to think of it, where had *she* come from? There was no door to a back room that I could see, just more shelves lining the rear wall, and if she'd been in the aisle, I'd definitely have noticed her.

"Jude said she's going to be late," Arthur was saying. "There are delays on the subway."

The blonde made a sound of disgust. "Of all days," she said. "Bryn Mawr had their annual book sale yesterday, and Lucille DePalma died."

What that had to do with being swamped with nonexistent book-buying customers I didn't know, but their being engaged in conversation gave me a chance to go look at the back of the store.

I'd been right—there wasn't a door. The shelves went all the way to the back wall and then turned the corner. The middle aisle of shelves ended a couple feet short of the wall, and I crossed over to the other side, but there was no door there either, just a spiral staircase leading up to a second floor and a sign with an arrow pointing up that read, "More books."

The blonde was coming back. I hurried back to where I'd been, grabbed a book off the shelves, and pretended to be looking at it. She passed me without a glance, walked over to the far side, and shot up the stairs, heels clattering on the metal steps. After a minute, I heard a door slam, and, curious, I went up the spiral staircase. The second floor looked exactly like the first except that the back wall was only half-covered with bookshelves. The other half was a door marked "Storeroom. Employees Only."

Which explained the "back there" comment. Except an upper floor was a peculiar place to store books, which are notoriously heavy. And what exactly would they be swamped with? Not preparing books for sale, since they didn't even bother to put a price in them, and I refused to believe they were swamped with orders. There hadn't been a computer—or even a phone—on the desk up front.

But she had made Jude's arrival sound desperately needed, and Arthur hadn't pooh-poohed her. What if Ozymandias's was a front for something else—a smuggling operation or a drug ring or black ops? That would explain how it could survive in the middle of Manhattan on the sale of fusty old copies of antiquated boys' books and Rex Stout mysteries. But if that were the case, Arthur would have discouraged me from looking around, wouldn't he? And the blonde wouldn't have advertised where she was going by slamming the door.

As I stood there trying to figure it out, I heard another door slam. It was somewhere behind this one and below it, and I wondered if instead of a storeroom behind the door, there was instead a stairway and the storeroom was down on the first floor after all, or in a basement. But why would the door to it be up on the second floor?

Maybe there was a door downstairs, but it's blocked by bookshelves, I thought. That was certainly more likely than some clandestine operation. And maybe the blonde always sounded urgent, and the work that was swamping her "back there" was a copy of *The Vagabond Boys Go to Carlsbad Caverns* that needed to be boxed up and taken to the post office.

But she'd said "we're" swamped, not "I," and she didn't look like the histrionic type. Her walk, her manner, her no-nonsense tone of voice had all denoted efficiency and organization. Boxing up the entire bookstore wouldn't have fazed her.

No, something else had to be going on, and after another minute, my curiosity got the best of me and I put my ear to the door for a moment, listening, and then tried the doorknob.

I'd expected the door to be locked, but it turned easily. *If it is a storeroom, and she's inside, I can always say I thought this was the bathroom*, I thought. But the shutting door I'd heard made me fairly sure she wouldn't be there.

She wasn't, and I was right, it wasn't a storeroom. The door opened onto a stairway leading down, and just the kind you'd expect behind a bookstore like this: a narrow, rickety, poorly-lit, Dickensian staircase with open wooden risers so you could see between them all the way down to the bottom. Where there was another door, just like I'd thought.

But I'd been wrong—the door didn't lead back into the bookstore. It was on the other side of the staircase, leading into whatever building lay behind the bookstore, and it wasn't on the first floor. The stairs zigzagged down at least two full floors between landings to reach it. And the blonde wasn't the one who I'd heard slamming the door because she was still in the stairwell, standing in front of the door talking to a chubby guy in a T-shirt and jeans. "When's Jude getting here?" he was asking.

"Soon, I hope," the blonde said, glancing up at the door behind me.

I ducked out of sight, thanking God I'd thought to shut the door and that the staircase was so dark, and crouched there, listening.

"She should be here in the next fifteen minutes or so," the blonde told the chubby guy. "Why? Did something happen?"

He nodded. "Tornado," he said grimly. "In Alabama. Town museum *and* the library."

"Oh, God," the blonde said, exasperated. "Just what we need. Was it a Carnegie?"

"Of course."

She sighed. "Can Greg stay late?"

"I'll ask," he said and disappeared through the door.

The blonde pulled out a cell phone and punched in a number. "Fran," she said into it, "Is there any chance you can come in? We're completely overwhelmed. Adelaide Westport died last week, and her niece flew in yesterday to clean out her house." A pause. "From Cupertino." Another pause. "It's in northern California."

And what the hell did this have to do with a tornado in Alabama—and what did either one have to do with selling *The Dionne Quintuplets in Hollywood?*

The blonde was still trying to persuade Fran to come in, even though a glance at my watch showed me it was nearly three o'clock and hardly worth the effort. Bookstores closed at five, didn't they?

"Well, can you think of anybody else?" she asked.

Apparently Fran couldn't because the blonde snapped her phone shut, stood there tapping her foot and looking down at her phone for a minute, and then went through the door.

As soon as it shut behind her, I racketed down the stairs, feeling like Alice chasing after the White Rabbit, and over to the door. As I put my hand on the doorknob, it occurred to me that what I was doing was beyond stupid. If Ozymandias's *was* a front for a smuggling operation or the NSA, then there were likely to be guns—or Bengal tigers—beyond that door.

But neither the blonde nor the chubby guy were criminal types, and spies didn't talk about Carnegie libraries and nieces from Cupertino even in code.

You don't know that, I thought as I turned the knob. *And if there* is *a Bengal tiger in there, nobody will ever know what happened to you. Nobody knows you're here.* I pulled out my phone to call Brooke and tell her, but I didn't have any coverage, and if I took the time to text her, I might lose the blonde.

There wasn't a tiger behind the door. There was another staircase. This one was neither rickety nor Dickensian. The steps were solid and cement and so were the walls, and it looked exactly like those stairwells in a parking garage, except that this one was brightly lit and clean, and there were books piled on nearly every step.

I went down a few steps till I was at eye-level with the stack on the top step. They seemed to be more of the peculiar mix that I'd seen in the store— *Remodeling Your Patio*, Edgar Allan Poe's *Deep in Earth*, Stewart Meredith Keane's *The Lone and Level Sands*, a biography of Rutherford B. Hayes, and a banged-up paperback of *Follow the Boys* with Connie Francis on the cover—and just as randomly organized. Maybe Ozymandias's didn't have a store-room, so this stairway had to double as one with the blonde sitting on one step and using another as a desk.

Or not. Because as I stood there, looking at the titles, I could hear the stacatto of the blonde's heels far below me, obviously going someplace. I took off down the stairs after her, trying not to make any noise and to calculate how far below me she was. Three levels at least, though the head of the stairs was already at basement level. Did Manhattan building foundations go down that far?

I doubted it. More likely, the cement walls were making it sound like she was farther away than she really was, and the bottom was only a single level below me.

It wasn't. I passed one landing and then another, and no floor, no blonde. Just lots more books, and, as I descended, more and more of them. At first there'd been only a single stack of half a dozen or so books on any given step. But as I went down, the stacks got higher and more numerous, and I had to work my way carefully between them so as not to knock one of them over and alert her to my presence.

Her clattering footsteps came to a stop far below me, and a heavy door slammed. I waited a minute to make sure she'd gone through it and then hurried down after her, no longer caring whether I made noise or knocked over some of the books. I didn't want to lose her.

The door she'd gone through had sounded like it was at least two flights below me, but either she was better at maneuvering between the maze of book piles or I'd misjudged the distance again, because by the time I made it down to the next door, the landing outside it and the steps below were completely blocked by books. There was no way I could make it down another dozen steps, let alone down another floor.

And there was no way she could have picked her way through these books quickly enough to have made it to the next landing. She *must* have gone through this door.

I worked my way to it, stepping over and around the piles of books, and pushed on the heavy handle.

It opened onto another staircase, almost as filled with stacks of books as the first one, but this one had open metal steps that zigzagged down at least two more floors into a vast, cavernous warehouse filled with aisle after aisle of books stretching in all directions for what seemed like miles.

I stared down at it, stunned. It was huge. It had to extend the length of the entire block, and, according to my calculations, it was at least five levels below the street. What the hell *was* this?

It must be a company like Amazon, which did most of its business by mail order. But if so, why hadn't I ever heard of it? And since when was there that big a market in used books? According to everybody I'd interviewed, public domain downloads of e-books and Google Books had cut into their sales so much that even Powell's was being forced out of business.

And if this was a mail-order operation, where were their shipping facilities? All I could see was Receiving, which consisted of a long metal slide that looked like a cross between a post office mail chute and an airport baggage carousel. Books were coming down it in a steady stream.

The blonde stood next to the carousel with a clipboard, supervising three burly workmen in overalls who were scooping the books up as they came down the chute and piling them onto big metal library carts. But not fast enough. The men were working at top speed, but they still weren't able to keep up. Books were piling up on the carousel and beginning to fall over the edge.

In my surprise, I had let go of the door, and it shut behind me. The blonde glanced up hopefully, as if she thought I might be the late-to-work Jude.

Shit. What would she—or worse, the burly workmen—do when they saw me? I backed against the door and felt for the handle, ready to make a quick getaway, but the blonde only looked disappointed that I wasn't Jude and then mildly annoyed. She started briskly over to the staircase, frowning. "What are you doing in here?" she called up to me. "This area is restricted to employees only."

I clattered down the steps to her. "The guy at the desk told me to come tell you that Jude had trouble getting a taxi. Because of the weather. Wow, this is some operation. How big is this place?"

"Not big enough," she said disgustedly. "Did he know how soon Jude would get here?"

"No."

"Oh, of all days for this to happen," she said, and at my questioning look, "We're absolutely swamped. Two used bookstores went out of business yesterday, and three libraries had their annual book sales."

"And you bought all the books that were left over?"

"No," she said.

They must have given them away. That would account for the motley assortment. "And you grabbed them for your bookstore to sell?" I said.

"This isn't a bookstore," she said.

26

I stared at her as if she were crazy. Not a bookstore? Then what the hell were all these books doing here?

"Then what is it?" I asked finally. "Some kind of library?" The New York Public Library was in midtown, wasn't it? Could this be some sort of storage annex? Or the place where they processed books that needed to be checked in? Though if the ones on the shelves I was standing next to were any indication, there wasn't much processing going on. They were as randomly shelved as the ones upstairs. An ancient-looking *New Theories of the Atom*, *The Vagabond Boys Go to Yosemite*, Sylvia Plath's *Double Exposure*, Iris R. Bracebridge's *The Daring Debutante*. "Is this part of the public library? Or or Columbia's library?"

"Hardly," she said scornfully. "Libraries are one of the biggest reasons we're here. Do you know how many books they destroy every year?"

"Destroy?" I said. "I thought librarians were all about preserving books."

"They believe that in principle," she said, "but in practice, they destroy hundreds of thousands of books a year. They don't call it that, of course. They call it 'retiring books' or 'pruning' or 'culling.' Or 'de-acquisition.'"

"De-acquisition?"

"Yes, it's supposed to sound like the benign counterpart of 'acquisition,' but it actually means getting rid of works that no longer 'serve the needs of the reading public.'"

Like The Daring Debutante *and half the books upstairs?* I thought, unconvinced that a little selective pruning was a bad thing. And it wasn't as if they were eradicating them. "Selling them isn't exactly destroying them," I said.

"They only sell a tiny percentage of them," she said, "and they're swamped with donations they can't use and not enough space for the books they already have, so most of the ones they discard end up getting sent to landfills—or recycling centers where they get pulped. And it never occurs to them that they might be the last copy of a book."

"And so the purpose of this place is to make sure that doesn't happen?" I asked, but she'd turned away to confer with one of the guys from the baggage carousel.

I didn't really need an answer. It was obvious from what she'd said and from the hodgepodge assortment of volumes coming down the chute that this place was some kind of home for books nobody else wanted, like those no-kill shelters for abandoned cats and dogs, and to a certain extent, I could sympathize. Much as I tout digitizing books, there's still something disturbing about the idea of shredding a physical book and/or dumping it in the trash. It's way too close to Hitler and his book-burnings for comfort.

But high-minded as the idea of saving orphaned books was, even an enterprise this size couldn't take in a fraction of the books that must get thrown out.

There were thousands of libraries in the country, not to mention all those independent bookstores the radio guy had said had closed. And she'd made it sound like they took in books from people who'd died, too. There was no way a single warehouse could accommodate all of those.

Though this place was bigger than I'd first thought, I realized, walking to the end of the row of bookshelves to peer down the cross-aisle. Rank after rank of crammed-full, twelve-foot-tall bookshelves stretched into the distance on either side of it.

What must the rent on this place be? And in mid-town Manhattan, too, let alone the equipment and the staff. Some eccentric book-loving millionaire must be bankrolling it. But if that was the case, why hadn't anybody heard of it?

"Stunning, isn't it?" the blonde said, coming back over to me. "Would you like a tour?"

"Yes," I said. "But I thought you said you were swamped."

"We're always swamped. Hang on another minute, and I'll get someone to cover for me." She walked over to the carousel, calling to the guys, "Were you able to get in touch with Anthony?"

"Yeah, and he said he'd try to get here, but he's over in Brooklyn, and the rain…"

"What about Thaddeus? Is he here?"

"Yeah. He's downstairs."

Downstairs? How many levels did this place have? I *definitely* wanted a tour.

"Well, tell him he needs to come up and fill in for me."

"But, Cassie, the Wallace estate sale just came in—"

Cassie, I thought, glad to know her name. Was it short for Cassandra?

"I know." she said. "Tell him it's only till Jude gets here, and that I'll send somebody down as soon as we finish with Mrs. DePalma's books." She didn't wait for me to answer. "I suppose it should be Libraries. I can show you what I've been talking about. Come this way."

She walked quickly along the bookshelves I'd been standing next to, gesturing toward the baggage chute and carousel as she went. "This is where the works come in, and these rows of shelves are where we store them till they can be catalogued."

She strode to the end of the row and turned down a cross-aisle which seemed to stretch for miles, with aisle after aisle of bookshelves.

"Wow," I said. "How many books—I mean, works, do you have here?"

"Too many," she said, and turned left into an aisle that looked exactly like the one back by the baggage chute, with the books just as randomly shelved. "This is still part of the unprocessed section, right?" I asked.

"No, this is Private Collections."

"You mean like the stuff they sell at Sotheby's?"
I asked. "Lord Such-and-Such's priceless collection
of first folios?" They didn't look like it. Half the
books appeared to be paperbacks or old textbooks,
and they certainly weren't leather-bound. Or organized in any way I could see. They definitely weren't
in alphabetical order. Or Dewey Decimal. I spotted
Shakespeare's *Cardenio* next to Irwin's *Maida's
Little Market* as we passed.

Cassie was still walking along the row. "We
occasionally acquire works from a bibliophile's or
a rare-book collector's estate, but the vast majority
come from books people had in their attics or cellars
or in an old trunk." She stopped next to a trio of
clothbound books. "These were Everett Hudson's, 34
Mott Street, Greenwich Village."

I remembered her talking about Mrs. DePalma
and Mrs. Westport dying. "He died?" I asked.

"No. Dementia. He had to be moved into a nurs-
ing home, and his only son lives in Tokyo and couldn't
get time off to come clean out his apartment and get it
ready to sell, so he hired a removal service to dispose
of the contents. And these," she said, pointing at the
books next to them, "came from a barn."

She leaned over, I thought to take one of the
books out to show me, and instead pulled out a stiff
manila card tucked like a bookmark between it and
Everett Hudson's books. "Barn, Rouse family farm,"

she said, reading from the neatly typed print on the card she was holding, "Clay County, Nebraska."

She tucked the card back in its place between the two groups of books and walked rapidly on, indicating various shelves as we passed. "These are from garages and attics and these over here are from hoarders."

Hoarders. I hadn't even thought about all the books they'd have, though whether they'd be salvageable was another question. I'd known a guy who was a hoarder. Between the dirt, the rat feces, the cat urine, and the mildew, I wouldn't have even wanted to set foot in his house, let alone scrabble through the disgusting mess for books. But from the number of shelves we passed, these people must have.

Unless these volumes were from some other kind of private collection. They had manila bookmarks dividing them, too, but there was no time to read their labels. Cassie was walking too quickly.

After several more aisles, she turned into a side aisle, went down two aisles, turned into the third, and stopped. "Here we are," she said.

"So these are the books the libraries got rid of to make room for Nicholas Sparks' latest romance novel?" I asked.

"Yes," she said bitterly, "plus the ones that didn't pass the double-fold test and the ones that were deemed to be 'too old,' as if books were like cartons of milk and had a sell-by date after which they went bad. And," she said, moving farther down the aisle, "the ones discarded during library relocations and renovations."

There were divider cards here, too, each with the name and location of the library and a date, presumably of when they'd acquired it. But what a bizarre way to catalog books: by the place they'd gotten it from. It had to be hopelessly inefficient.

Though Cassie seemed to know where every single one was. "Blackthorne Public Library," she said, without even looking at the identifying cards. "Lincoln Park Library, Franklin County Library."

"Nothing from the Library of Alexandria?" I asked jokingly.

She didn't even crack a smile. "We're English language only," she said. "And they wouldn't be in this section anyway. They'd be in Fires."

No, they wouldn't, I thought, because the whole place had gone up in flames. There hadn't been anything left to save.

"East Lake Library in Paul Harbor, Florida," Cassie was saying, pointing at sections. "Mitchell Library in Sydney, Australia, Golden Library at Eastern New Mexico State University—"

"University? Colleges and universities de-acquisish, or whatever it's called, too?"

"Yes, especially since the advent of InterLibrary Loan. They assume their students can borrow the work from some other library, so there's no reason to keep their own copy, and it doesn't occur to them till too late that theirs might be the only one. And Project Gutenberg and Google Books have made it even worse."

Oh, here we go, I thought. "You don't approve of digitizing books."

"Oh, no, I'm grateful for it. Without it, we'd be even more swamped. But the libraries assume that *all* books are online and that therefore they don't need to have a physical copy, and they dispose of theirs. Only they're *not* all online. Just a fraction of them are. And there's also the problem of data corruption. And of putting books onto microfilm, which cracks and deteriorates, or into a digital format which can be accessed only through technological means, and then those means becoming obsolete, like the floppy disk or 12-inch video disks, like they did with *The Domesday Book*. Putting books on an inaccessible platform is nearly as effective at destroying books as the shredder."

I was afraid from here she'd go off on accidental deletions and the dangers of putting all your eggs in one basket like the guy at WMNH had. I said hastily, "But there's always the Cloud. And the Library of Congress. They have a copy of every book that's been published in the U.S., right?"

She shook her head. "They didn't start doing that till the 1860s, and more than seventy thousand works are lost to decay and disintegration every year. Plus, they've had three major fires, with a combined loss of three hundred thousand volumes," she said, "quite a lot of it due to the water damage that occurred when trying to put out the fires. Water damage is the second most common cause of book destruction."

"What's first?" I asked, but she'd already turned down another aisle.

"Water damage is along here," she said. "Leaky roofs, broken plumbing, flooded basements. And down there are the floods—the Ohio River, the Republican River, Yancey Creek, North Carolina..."

I looked at the books as we passed. Most of the sections had only two or three books, and Yancey Creek had just one, which was, fittingly enough, *Noah's Ark on Ararat.*

It didn't have any signs of water damage I could see, and neither did any of the other books, which meant they had to have been subject to some kind of advanced salvage technique.

I revised my theory of eccentric millionaire up to billionaire. Technologies to salvage waterlogged books cost big money. I'd researched the big 1966 flood of the Arno which had destroyed Florence's National Library, in connection with a pro-digitizing post I'd written. Their vacuum freeze-drying and other book-salvaging equipment had been wildly expensive.

Or maybe these were just the few that hadn't gotten soaked.

"Flash floods," Cassie said. "Sheffield; Big Thompson; Rapids City, South Dakota; Fort Collins, Colorado." She paused a moment to indicate a shelf of books. "That one was particularly bad because the university library was being remodeled and all the Colorado history books and doctoral dissertations had been moved to the basement."

Which explained why the books all had titles like *Irrigation Techniques in Use in Dryland Farming* and *The Narrow Gauge Railroad in the Rocky Mountains from 1871 – 1888.*

"Landslides," Cassie said, still walking, not even glancing at the bookmarks as she passed, "mudslides, sinkholes."

Shelving the books this way, by the agent of their almost-demise, was crazy, but it certainly highlighted the dangers facing books. Just like a nature preserve putting up signs telling what had decimated the particular species: poaching, acid rain, loss of habitat, pesticides.

There seemed to be just as many ways to wipe out books. As we walked, Cassie pointed out sections for censorship, changes in taste, academic trends.

"Academic trends?" I said.

"Yes. Some authors, like Dreiser and Alexander Pope, go out of favor with academics and are no longer taught. Or a book's wildly popular and then just as quickly goes out of print and is forgotten."

"Like *The Bridges of Madison County*, you mean?" I said, hoping they weren't trying to rescue it. It was the perfect example of all those things society was better off without.

"Not yet," she said. "I mean books like *The Sheik* and Elinor Glyn's novels. And Charlotte Yonge's."

"Charlotte Yonge? I've never heard of her."

"Exactly. At one time she was the most popular author in England, even outselling Dickens. And now no one even recognizes her name. And then there are books that disappear because they've become out-moded or discredited, like *Dirigibles: Our Future*, and *Using Your K+E Slide Rule*."

Or that surviving the Y2K apocalypse book, I thought.

"Or because they're badly dated," Cassie was saying, "like *Flossie and Her School Friends* and *Ambush in Apache Canyon*—"

Ambush in Apache Canyon?

Finally, a book worth saving. "I remember reading that when I was a kid," I told Cassie. "It was my favorite book. My uncle gave it to me. I'd kill to read it again."

I had no idea what had happened to it. Could my mom have given it to the library and it had ended up in this place?

"You have a copy of *Ambush in Apache Canyon* here?" I asked Cassie.

There was a pause, as if she thought I might try to steal it if she said yes, which convinced me it *was* my copy, and then nodded. "Would you like to see it?"

"Yeah," I said, looking over at the books, searching for the blue and brown and red cover.

"It's not here," she said. "It's in the Children's section."

Oh, of course. That made sense. Kids' books would end up in library discard piles and estate sales and attics, too.

"That's over here," Cassie said and led the way quickly down four rows, over an aisle, down another two rows to another aisle in a zig-zagging trail just like the one the kid had followed through the red rock canyons in *Ambush in Apache Canyon*, searching for the missing cattle. Except he'd ended up trapped in a box canyon with a band of Apaches leaping suddenly out at him from the rocks.

God, I'd loved that book. It had had everything a boy of nine could want—horses, six-shooters, war paint, cattle rustlers, the cavalry riding to the rescue. But I wasn't surprised it had ended up in a library sale. Westerns had already been old hat in my uncle's day, and as I recalled, the book had been full of politically incorrect language like "marauding wild Indians" and "red savages."

And the book had been cheaply printed, on that paper that turns brown and brittle in a matter of

months. It had already been in bad shape when my
uncle gave it to me—the dust jacket torn, the bind-
ing half-detached, the pages coming loose—and in
even worse shape by the time I'd finished reading it.
Definitely a candidate for the landfill.

And no doubt the radio interview guy would cite this
as an example of good things being lost, but it wasn't. It
was here, which was proof that if society needed something, it found a way to make sure it survived.

Cassie had gotten a long ways ahead of me. I hurried to catch up before she disappeared down one of
the rows and I lost her. "Is this Children's?" I asked as
I approached her and she turned into an aisle.

But it clearly wasn't. No picture books, or fairy
tales, just more of the same kind of thing in all
the other sections: Macleod's *Trout Fishing in the
Hebrides*, Milton's *Adam Unparadis'd*, Henry Calvin
Russell's *Marooned on Saturn*, P.T. Hicks' *Chickens
is Chickens*, even what had to be another doctoral
dissertation, *Microbial Biosynthesis in Karstic
Sediments* by Darryl A. Krauss, Ph. D. Not exactly
Dr. Seuss.

"So how much farther to Children's?" I asked.

"This is it," Cassie said, and began pointing
out divider cards. "Peanut butter. Spilled Kool-Aid.
Melted chocolate."

Oh, books *destroyed* by children. Of course. I'd
forgotten their weird method of categorizing.

And now that I looked closer, I saw that there were some children's books sandwiched in among the others. I spotted *The Tale of Little Flinders* and *Tommy Todd's Birthday Surprise* and L. Frank Baum's *Molly Oodle* and *The Vagabond Boys Go To the Blue Ridge Mountains*. Jesus, how many of those damned Vagabond Boys books were there?

"Left on the beach," Cassie went on, ticking off the sections as she moved down the row. "Left on the bleachers, played catch with—"

"Dropped in the bathtub," I put in, remembering the incident that had made me decide to get a Kindle.

"Yes," Cassie said, continuing along the row. "Spitup. Teething. Torn up by a toddler. Colored in. Scribbled in with Magic Marker—"

Which would be even harder to remove than the stains of water damage, I thought, pausing to see how they'd gotten that out, but before I could look at it, Cassie called from the end of the row, "Here it is!" She held up a book.

Even from that far away I instantly recognized it. The blue and brown cover with the boy on horseback picking his way between the narrow, red-rock walls of the canyon was exactly the same as the one on my copy, but it definitely wasn't my book. This copy looked like new, the dust cover untorn, the colors unfaded.

"That's it, all right," I said happily. "Just like I remembered it. Have you read it?"

"No," she said, "it just came in," and put *Ambush* back on the shelf. "I was going to show you the Fires section," she said, heading across the aisle and then over to another cross-aisle and down it, pointing out the various sections: "Earthquakes, Volcanic eruptions, Shipwrecks."

And how exactly had they managed to recover those? A submarine thing like the one they'd used on the *Titanic*? And was the *Titanic* one of the ships she was talking about? It had had everything—a gym, a bowling alley, a post office—which probably meant it had had a lending library, too.

I asked Cassie if it had.

"Yes," she said promptly. "Four hundred volumes, plus the books the passengers and crew brought along with them—including Selden's *Modern Ocean Travel* and *The Plight of the Vicar's Daughter*, which we have here, and a priceless jeweled copy of *The Rubaiyat of Omar Khayyam*."

Wow. "Is it here, too?"

Cassie looked taken aback. "No, of course not. There are still thousands of copies of the *Rubaiyat* in existence." She bit her lip. "I don't think you understand what this facility—" she began and then stopped, looking over my shoulder.

I turned. One of the guys who'd been unloading books from the baggage carousel was standing three aisles back with a clipboard and a worried expression.

"What is it, Greg?" Cassie called to him.

"Problem," he said, waving the clipboard at her.

"Sorry," Cassie said to me. "I'll be right back," and started toward him reluctantly, as if she wished she could finish saying what she'd been telling me first.

But I'd already figured it out. This wasn't a no-kill shelter for books that had been thrown out. It was an endangered-book archive, like those gorilla and elephant sanctuaries or those repositories for rare types of seeds, to keep them from going extinct. And it was the scarcity of a book that determined its place here, not its collectible value or literary quality.

The books here were the last of their kind, or close to it. Which meant that my falling-apart copy of *Ambush in Apache Canyon*—and all the other copies—must have been thrown out. Or washed away or burned up or de-acquisished by some librarian to make room for more copies of *Harry Potter.*

But at least there was still a copy here. And it proved that what I'd told the radio interview guy was true—that if something had value, society would find a way to keep it around.

Ambush in Apache Canyon definitely deserved to survive, though I wasn't sure Leonardo DiCaprio did, or *Flossie and Her School Friends.* Or all those doctoral dissertations.

But it explained why they were here. Only a handful of copies of those had ever existed. A flood could have cut the numbers in half.

What it didn't explain was why they hadn't recovered the jeweled *Rubaiyat* and sold it to finance this place. Which had to cost a fortune. We'd walked what?—half a mile?—already and were no closer to the end that I could see.

"Sorry," Cassie said, coming back. "We just got hit with another deluge. Bookstore closing." She shook her head. "We were already overwhelmed, and now this."

I was afraid this was leading up to her saying she'd have to cut the tour short, but she didn't. She started off again in the direction we'd been headed before, still talking over her shoulder to me. "And as if that's not bad enough, Jude called and said she's going to be at least another half hour. It's apparently still raining hard outside, and the subway's flooded. I told Greg to tell her to take a taxi, and we'd reimburse her, but I'm afraid she won't be able to find one," she said, sounding worried.

She should be worrying about this *place instead*, I thought, tagging after her. We were at least as far below ground as the subway system. A warehouse like this was likely to flood, too, and she had to know the danger, what with the survivors of all those past floods on the shelves we'd just passed.

But Cassie's main concern seemed to be how long it would take for Jude to get there if she had to walk. "The taxis all vanish whenever it rains!" she said.

I looked down toward the end of the cross-aisle, but we were too far away from any walls for me to see if they were wet. I looked down at the floor. It was bone-dry, and I couldn't see any puddles, or worse, trickles of water in the aisles. But I couldn't see any pumps, either.

They must have some sort of built-in water-proofing—floodgates or something. But I remembered, post-Sandy, seeing photos of a flood-proofed, temperature-controlled, top-security wine cellar for rare vintages. The priceless bottles had been bobbing in six feet of water, their labels floating beside them.

And since they'd already had to dry these books out once, you'd think they'd at least be checking for leaks—or be setting in motion a plan for moving the books upstairs if necessary.

I hated to admit the radio guy who'd interviewed me was right about anything, but this place was another Wheeler's Field waiting to happen.

But Cassie was only worried about Jude getting here *now* to deal with the books coming in from this latest bookstore's closing. "It's Elliott's," Cassie said, which was the one the radio interview guy had mentioned. "It had been there since 1899."

Translation: it had a bunch of old books that might be endangered. I wondered exactly how they figured out which ones they needed to bring here. Was that the job of the old guy at the desk upstairs in the store?

But one person wouldn't be enough for a job like that. Finding out how many copies of *Fairy Tales for Wee Tots* or *The Vagabond Boys Go to Mount Shasta* were left in the world would take tons of research. And how exactly would you go about it?

I wanted to ask Cassie, but she was still going on about Elliott's' closing. "There used to be other bookstores who could buy up their stock when one closed," she said, "but now, with so many having already gone under, there's no one who can take them and see to it they survive."

"Except you," I noted, but she'd already taken off again, saying, "I want to show you the Fires section."

"Fires?" I said, getting a sudden upsetting image of Cassie charging into a burning building to rescue books.

But she had her hands full here. There must be a whole other team—or teams—who did that, and that went and picked up the books from all those houses and storage units and bankrupt bookstores. Plus researchers to determine whether a book qualified as endangered. I upped my estimate of the cost of this enterprise another digit.

"Fire's one of our biggest sections," Cassie stopped to say. "As you can imagine. Lightning-caused fires, faulty wiring, arson, playing with matches, accident, civil disobedience. Or both."

"Both?"

She nodded. "The Michigan State Library fire was caused by a student trying to burn the state draft board files so he wouldn't be drafted and ended up destroying twenty thousand volumes."

She started to walk again and then stopped, and I saw she was standing in front of a divider labeled "Dresden."

"So this is the Fires section?" I asked, gesturing at it.

"No," she said. "War. But there's considerable overlap. That's why they're shelved next to each other. These rows are High-Explosive Bombs," she said, walking me quickly past several rows, rattling off the names of the bombed buildings as she went: "Westminster Abbey Chapter Library, Allen and Unwin, Holland House, Lambeth Palace, the British Museum Reading Room—"

"My God, how big is this section?" I asked.

"Big," she said. "Twenty million volumes were destroyed by bombs in the London Blitz alone."

"So is war the biggest?"

She turned to look back at me. "The biggest?"

"Cause of book destruction. You said water damage was the second biggest. Is war the first?"

"No."

"Then what is?"

For a second I thought she wasn't going to answer me, and then she said, "Time."

"Time?"

She nodded. "Decay. Paper deterioration, ink degradation, glue oxidation, overuse."

"Overuse?"

"Being read so many times the book falls to pieces."

Like I'd done with *Ambush in Apache Canyon*. I could see its browning, brittle pages and its broken spine in my mind's eye.

"Bookworms," she said. "Dry rot, moths, mildew, mold. And attrition."

"Attrition?"

"The gradual destruction of one copy after another over the years through a whole variety of circumstances. The ravages of time."

I could see that. One copy lost at sea, another chewed up by the family dog, others sent to the landfill and put on no-longer-readable microfilm, and pretty soon there would be hardly any left.

"It doesn't affect us here as much as at the other branches because English hasn't been around as long as some languages," Cassie said, "but it's still our number one cause. Though war certainly contributes. These books are from the Library of Louvain."

"It was bombed?"

"Yes, but not by the enemy. The Library's Tower provided a landmark for the gunners to adjust their sights by, so the defenders destroyed it."

She walked on. "This next section is Paper Drives. During World War II, they collected scrap paper to make into ammunition, including, unfortunately, old books. And this next section is—"

"Wait—other *branches?*"

"Yes. I told you, we're English language only."

"So how many other branches are there? And where—?"

"Cassie?" a male voice called from the cross-aisle. "Where are you?"

"Here, Greg," she called back, and the guy from before appeared at the end of the row, looking apologetic.

"Don't tell me," she said. "Jude can't find a taxi."

"Yeah, she said she's been trying for fifteen minutes and there's not a one to be found, so she's going to have to walk it, and, in the meantime, we've got another problem."

Aha! I thought. *This place* is *leaking.*

But Greg said, "Today's the twenty-first."

"You're kidding!" Cassie said. "I completely forgot."

"We've *got* to get more people in here to help with it," Greg said, "and I've called everybody I can think of."

"What about Rita?"

"She said she's already worked overtime every day this week, and—"

"I'll talk to her," Cassie interrupted. She turned to me. "Sorry, I need to go take care of this. I'll be back in a minute," she said and hurried off with Greg, while I wandered along the War aisles, wondering what was special about the twenty-first and looking at the books and the divider cards—Sarajevo National Library, Bosnian War; Library of Strasbourg, Franco-Prussian War; Library of Congress, War of 1812—Jesus, how long had they been doing this?—and then, since she still wasn't back, went on to see if I could find the Fires section on my own.

She was right about the overlap. There were a half-dozen rows of shelves marked "Fire-Bombings" and "Incendiaries" and two more that, judging by their dates, could have been either, and then fires that had clearly been civilian—the Windsor Castle fire, 1992; the Capitol Fire in Albany, 1911, Birmingham Central Library in 1879...

The sections were all small here, too, including sections like "Los Angeles Public Library Fire," which I remembered as doing major damage. But apparently only a handful of them had been books that were rare enough that they qualified for archiving here.

Or that was all they'd managed to rescue. I walked down the rows to see if I could find a section with more books in it.

Here was one. It took up two full shelves and half of a third. I peered at the divider card to see where these books had come from. "St. Paul's," it read.

St. Paul's? Didn't these books belong over in the War section with the other London Blitz stuff? That was when Hitler had tried to burn the cathedral down.

But he hadn't succeeded. St. Paul's hadn't burned. So why was this section here? This must be some other St. Paul's—St. Paul's Catholic School or St. Paul's College or the St. Paul, Minnesota Public Library.

If the titles were any indication, it must be. The titles weren't those of religious books—John Ogilbie's *The Carolies,* Sir William Dugdale's *Origines Judiciales*, *The History of Embanking and Draining*, Sir Thomas Urquhart's *The Jewel*... And anyway, what books would St. Paul's Cathedral have besides hymnals and tourist guides?

I pulled out the divider card to take a closer look. No, it read, "St. Paul's Cathedral, London," and there was only one of those. It must have been hit by some incendiary bomb at some point that caused a minor fire. But that still didn't explain what all these secular books had been doing in a cathedral.

"And call Terence," Cassie's voice said. "Tell him we'll pay him double overtime," and heard the tap of her heels coming toward me. I went out to meet her.

"Sorry," she said. "It never rains but it pours. California just changed the period of time before unclaimed storage units can be legally auctioned off. It used to be three months, which meant the first, but they just changed it to twelve weeks, so now they hold the auctions on the twenty-first."

"Storage units? Like on that TV show, *Storage Wars?*" I asked. "Where dealers bid on the contents and then sell them?"

"Or try to, can't find any takers, and then toss them in the dumpster," she said grimly. She turned to look at the books. "I see you found the Fires section."

"Yeah," I said, nodding. "And I think I found some mis-shelved books."

"Mis-shelved?" she repeated in a tone that said clearly, "That's impossible." She came over. "Which ones?"

I led the way down the row to the St. Paul's section. "These. They're marked 'St. Paul's Cathedral.' Shouldn't they be over in the World War II section?"

"No," she said, without even looking at the divider. "These are from the Great Fire of London in 1665."

"Oh."

"The booksellers and publishers in the surrounding area moved their books into the cathedral for safekeeping."

Which had obviously been a good idea, considering how much of the rest of London the fire had destroyed. Including, apparently, most—or all—of the other copies of these books, since there were so many of them here. And it made sense that Ozymandias's would have known they were the last copies when they acquired them—they'd have had hundreds of years to check on their rarity.

But it didn't explain how they could afford them—the last extant copy of a book from the 1600s would have been pricey even for a billionaire, and they'd have had to outbid the Folger and the British Library, and there were dozens of them here—or why, if they were as priceless as I thought they had to be, they were just sitting out there on the shelves for the taking instead of being locked in burglar-proof cases.

And it didn't explain how they knew the rest of the books here—*The Daring Debutante* and *Follow the Boys* and *Ambush in Apache Canyon*—qualified as endangered, how they knew there weren't dozens of other copies stashed in barns and hoarders' houses and storage units people were still paying rent on.

"How exactly do you select the books for this place?" I said.

"Select?" Cassie repeated blankly.

"Yeah. How do you know if a book you find is the last copy of something? Is there a master list of endangered books somewhere or—?"

Cassie put up her hand to silence me, her head cocked as if listening, and after a couple of seconds I knew what had made her do that. The sound of footsteps.

"Greg? We're down here," Cassie called, and a head appeared around the corner of our row. But not Greg's.

It was a young woman who *had* to be the long-awaited Jude. She looked like a drowned rat, her clothes plastered to her and great drops of water dripping from her black bangs.

"I'm here," she told Cassie breathlessly. "What do you want me to do first?"

Get out of those wet clothes before you drip all over the books, I thought.

But Cassie didn't even seem to notice her soaking wet clothes or the puddle she was standing in. "Go down to Manuscripts and ask Jerome if he has any rolling carts he can spare and then start clearing the chute," she said.

Jude nodded and left, only to reappear a moment later, saying, "I forgot to tell you. Thaddeus says he needs to talk to you. It's about Lewis Carroll's diaries. He wants to know if he should shelve them under Carroll or Dodgson."

"Tell him—"

"And he had a question about Volumes 6 and 7. He said it's really urgent."

Cassie nodded. "All right, tell him I'll be right there." She looked regretfully at me. "I'm sorry I have to keep abandoning you like this. If you want to—"

Call it quits? Not till you tell me how this place works and how you can afford something like Lewis

Carroll's diaries, I thought. *And why, in a section devoted to books that were nearly destroyed once in a fire, you don't have a single fire extinguisher.*

"It's okay," I said. "I've got plenty of time. You go. I'll entertain myself by looking at bookburnings or something."

Which was supposed to be a joke, but it went over as well as my joke about the Library of Alexandria.

"They're four rows down," Cassie said seriously. "Near the middle. Second shelf from the bottom," and went off with the still-dripping Jude.

I went off to find the bookburnings section, wondering what I'd find. Probably not Hitler's infamous bonfires—this was English-language only, and he'd burned mostly German and Polish books. And besides, there'd have been no way to rescue them.

Then what would they be? Fundamentalist burnings of *Harry Potter* or the Koran? No, neither one would qualify as endangered. Slave records that would incriminate prominent Southern families? I'd read about a recent case in North Carolina where they'd burned a bunch of those. Or would they be Salman Rushdie's books? Or Darwin's?

It didn't matter, because I couldn't find the section at all. It wasn't anywhere in the fourth row, or the fifth, which was devoted entirely to arson. I backtracked to the third to look, but it seemed to be all garden-variety non-arson fires—schools, houses, businesses: the offices of the *Liberty Review*, Maysburg Elementary School, Kenyon Dormitory—

Dormitory. I stopped, frowning at the card, remembering a dorm fire when I'd been in college.

It hadn't been a big one. Only a couple of rooms had been damaged before they got it out, but the whole floor (and the one above it) had had to throw everything out. The smell of smoke had penetrated not only the clothes and blankets and mattresses, but everybody's textbooks, their furniture, even the walls. And not the nice outdoorsy smell you get from a campfire either—an overwhelming, sickening reek. I leaned over the books and sniffed.

Nothing. I walked back along the row and back up the aisle to the St. Paul's books, taking periodic whiffs.

Still nothing.

The smell of smoke had been impossible to get out. They'd tried everything: washing, dry cleaning, repainting, buckets of industrial strength odor-remover, but nothing had worked. It was still there.

And yet here I was, supposedly surrounded on all sides by rows and rows of books that had been rescued from fires, and there wasn't the slightest hint of smoke.

These people have technologies for de-mudding books and rescuing them from the bottom of the ocean, I told myself. *Maybe they've got one for getting rid of smoke.*

But even if they had, there should have been a lingering whiff of it left, with all these thousands of books. Just like there should have been a smell of cordite in the War section and of damp over in Water Damage. And in the rest of it, that musty dust-and-decay smell that's part and parcel of every old bookstore and library. I'd never been in one that didn't have it. Except this place.

Okay, so maybe it was temperature- and atmosphere-controlled, which would seem to be a requirement with all these irreplaceable books, but I could see no indication of that, just like there was no sign of any sprinkler system or smoke alarms. Which safety regulations required, along with emergency lighting and exit signs.

Which I couldn't see anywhere either.

Don't be ridiculous, I thought. *They're just too far away for you to see them.*

Even though we'd come what felt like miles, I was no closer to the end of the facility than I had been. And maybe now, with Cassie gone, would be the perfect opportunity to see exactly how big this place was.

I took a quick look back to make sure she wasn't returning yet and set off down the cross-aisle, counting rows so I wouldn't get lost, and intending to go all the way to the far wall. But thirty rows later I was no closer, and ahead the way was blocked by one of those big warehouse loaders, filled with pallets full of books.

I had to go over a row to the next aisle, only to run into a grilled-off area filled with what looked like stacks of old ledgers.

I went down several rows, looking for a way around it, without success, and then decided I'd better go back to Fires before I got lost.

Too late. I'd thought I'd kept track of the number of aisles and cross-aisles I'd come, but I must have lost track at some point. I couldn't find Fires *or* War—the books here were all weather-related disasters—hurricanes, tornados, tsunamis—and in the row I'd have sworn I'd started from, there was a Post-it note stuck to a shelf that read, "Cassandra, these works were donated by a library to a school in Bangladesh. Should they be shelved in culling or typhoon?" that I was positive I'd have noticed if I'd been here before.

I must have gone over three aisles instead of two. I walked back another, and another, but there was still no Fires section—and no sign of Cassie. And no sound of anybody coming.

The thought came to me, like it had on the staircase coming down here, that nobody had any idea I was here. And that if this wasn't a nature preserve for books, if it was something else—a front for drug-smuggling or armaments dealing or something even more bizarre—that they didn't want anybody to find out about, that they wouldn't need to cosh me over the head or brick me up in a wall, like a character in an Edgar Allen Poe story. All they had to do was abandon me in the middle of this labyrinth like Cassie just had, with no bread crumbs and no map. And no way to call for help, because this far underground, there couldn't possibly be any cell phone coverage.

And there wasn't, not a single bar. I walked several aisles over and one down, holding the phone up, trying to get some reception, but I didn't get anything, and it came to me belatedly that by wandering around I was making things worse. If Cassie *hadn't* left me here to die, she'd expect me to be where she'd left me or close to it.

I had no idea where that was or even what direction Cassie had gone in when she left with Jude. Or which way the baggage carousel lay from here. All I could see on every side, stretching away into the distance, was aisle after aisle of bookshelves that all looked exactly alike.

There must be something I could orient myself by—a book's distinctive color or its title—but I didn't see anything I recognized.

The puddle Jude's wet shoes and dripping clothes made, I thought, and went quickly along the aisle I was in, and then the next, looking for wetness on the floor of the cross-aisles, but either it had dried or in trying to reach the wall I'd gone farther afield than I'd thought.

Or I was going in circles. Which was entirely possible, given the sameness of the shelves of books. I needed to find a way to mark my path so I'd at least know where I'd been. I fumbled in my pants pocket, looking for change—or lint or something I could use as breadcrumbs, but all my pockets yielded was a dime and two pennies, and there wasn't anything here to use.

What was I saying? The shelves were chock full of breadcrumbs—*Heartbreak Summer* and *How to Write a Thriller in Five Days* and, especially appropriate, *Following in the Master's Footsteps*. I could leave a trail of them on the floor to mark which direction I was going and where I'd already been.

I was reaching for Mme. Shirotsky's *Visitations from Beyond the Veil* when I thought I heard something. I went out into the cross-aisle to listen and heard the unmistakable click of Cassie's heels, though I still couldn't see her. And she wouldn't be looking for me here, wherever here was.

"Cassie?" I called, and at the same instant, my phone rang.

I stared at it. It still wasn't showing any bars, and I knew there couldn't be any coverage down here, but there was, and when I answered it, Brooke's voice was clearer than it had been on the street outside WMNH.

"I've been trying to get you for half an hour," she said. "Where are you?" and before I could answer, "Never mind. It doesn't matter. What matters is that you get yourself over to Random House. Your meeting's back on."

"I thought he'd left for London."

"They cancelled his flight because of the weather. He's got a seat on the eleven-ten. Which means he can see you. If you can get there in the next fifteen minutes, that is. You can do that, can't you?"

"I don't know," I said, thinking of how long it would take me to get back to the baggage carousel—assuming Cassie got here to show me the way—and then to run up all those flights of stairs to the bookshop.

"What do you mean?" Brooke said. "Please don't tell me you're out in Brooklyn or at the Statue of Liberty or something."

"No, I'm in Midtown," I said, "but—"

"Oh, good. I'll tell him you're on your way. Bye."

"No, wait! Before you hang up, I need to tell you where I am. I stopped in this bookstore called Ozymandias—" but I was talking to dead air. She'd already ended the call.

Shit, shit, shit. I hit redial. I got a "call cannot be completed" screen, and before I could try again, Cassie appeared at the far end of the cross-aisle.

"Sorry," she said. "There was an earthquake in La Jolla. Did you think I was never coming back?"

"Listen, I'm afraid I've got to leave," I said. "I just got a call from my agent. She set up an appointment for me with a publisher—"

"Oh, too bad," she said. "I wanted to show you the Thefts and Vandalism section. Are you sure you don't have time to—?"

"Afraid not," I said. "It's in fifteen minutes."

"I understand," she said and started briskly back up the cross-aisle the way she'd come.

I followed her. "It's at Broadway and 56th," I said doubtfully. "Do you think I'll be able to make it in time?"

"Your appointment's at four?" she said, turning down a side-aisle. "That shouldn't be a problem."

Good, I thought as she made another turn. *That means there's one of those loaders nearby*, but none appeared, and she seemed to be heading in the opposite direction of the way she'd come.

"Are you sure—?" I began.

She nodded. "You can take the elevator."

Elevator? I thought, following her. *What elevator?* There hadn't been an elevator in the bookstore. But here was one.

"This'll take you to street level," she said, pushing the button on the wall beside it.

The door opened immediately on a large freight elevator full of rolling carts stacked with books. There was barely space for me to squeeze in.

"I'm sorry to rush off like this," I said, wedging myself between two of the carts. "Can I take a raincheck on the rest of the tour? Or I guess it should be a fair-weather check. I really want to see all of this. It's an amazing place."

"Yes," she said, reaching inside to push one of the buttons on the panel and then stepping back out of the elevator. "It is."

"Is there a time that's good?" I asked. "Some time when you aren't so busy?"

She shook her head. "There's no such time," she said, and before I could say anything else, the door slid shut and the elevator started moving.

Let's hope it's not as slow as most freight elevators, I thought, and the elevator gave a groan and lurched to a stop.

Not now, I thought. There went the interview. I reached for the red emergency button.

There wasn't one, and none of the buttons on the panel were numbered.

I looked at my phone—no bars—and it occurred to me, too late, that an elevator would make an even better trap than that labyrinth of books, in which case yelling, "Get me out of here!" wasn't going to do any good.

Neither would pushing the buttons, but I jabbed at them anyway, and, after a long, panicky moment, the door began to slide open.

I peered cautiously out, afraid of what might be out there. More endless rows of shelves? Or something worse?

No, but it wasn't the bookstore either. I was in an old-fashioned office-building lobby of greenish marble. *This must be the building next door to Ozymandias's*, I thought. Or, considering how long those aisles had been, several doors down.

I could see through the fancy glass-and-grillwork revolving door at the front of the lobby that it was getting dark and still raining hard. I could also see a taxi sitting out front, and wonder of wonders, it had its light on.

I shot through the lobby, out the revolving door, and into the cab. "Can you get me to 1745 Broadway in ten minutes?" I said, even though I saw now that the reason he'd been sitting there was that traffic was completely gridlocked. "There's fifty bucks in it for you if you can."

"You got it," he said, and maneuvered the cab into a nonexistent right-hand lane, and raced past a truck and down the street, missing a woman with an umbrella by millimeters, and a bicycle messenger by less than that.

When I was able to breathe again, I looked back to try and see where I'd come out and determine how far it was from the bookshop, but we'd already turned the corner and were moving up a side street.

Which one? Sixth Avenue? Seventh? I tried to spot a sign so I'd know which street the bookshop had been on, but the rain was turning into snow, and between that and the darkness, streaked with red and green and orange light, it was impossible to make out what the ones we passed said.

I gave up, texted Brooke to tell Random House I was on my way, but it was going to be close because of the traffic, and then looked up which side of the street it was on so the driver could drop me in front of it and maybe save a couple of minutes, and by the time I'd finished telling him, "It's on the west side, in the middle," we were at the Ninth Avenue and 55th, a fact I knew because the traffic had slowed to a dead stop right in front of the sign.

Three blocks away. And it was 4:53. I peered out at the sleet, wondering if I should get out and make a run for it, but, based on the pedestrians I saw, I'd freeze before I got there, and the cabbie was already turning into a nonexistent gap and bulling his way up the street.

He pulled up in front of Random House with nanoseconds to spare. I thrust three twenties at him and opened the door.

"You want a recei—?" he began.

"No," I said, and flung myself out of the taxi, across the wet sidewalk, and into the building. Only to find that the editor was already gone.

"He was able to get a flight out of Newark," the receptionist told me. "He said to tell you he was sorry about making you come all this way and that he'd text you."

He did. "SORRY TO CANCEL. HAD A CHANCE AT ANOTHER FLIGHT AND THOUGHT I'D BETTER TAKE IT. STORM'S SUPPOSED TO GET WORSE. WILL RESCHEDULE."

And a couple of minutes later, "LISTENED TO YOUR WMNH INTERVIEW. YOUR COMMENTS WERE GREAT. DEFINITELY WANT TO MEET WITH YOU ABOUT DOING BOOK."

And immediately after that, "ESPECIALLY LIKED THE WHOLE 'GOODBYE AND GOOD RIDDANCE,' THING. AND THE FACT THAT BOOKS ARE IN NO DANGER OF DISAPPEARING."

I'm not sure that's true, I thought, remembering that deluge of endangered books pouring down the conveyor belt, and was about to text him about it, but he'd already sent, "Have to go. Boarding," and besides, it would be more impressive to hit him with the whole story of the book preserve and how it worked, so I texted, "Bon voyage," and then went back into the sleet, which was rapidly turning into snow, and tried to find a taxi to take me to Fiada's.

There wasn't a taxi to be found, and ten minutes later an assistant from Tor called to tell me they were canceling the dinner because of the weather, followed by a call from HarperCollins doing the same thing with the meetup for drinks.

I was just as glad. Getting another taxi seemed to be out of the question, I was freezing, and all I wanted to do was get out of these drenched clothes, get something to eat, and go to bed. Because if I was going to write about Ozymandias's operation, I needed to go back there first thing tomorrow morning and get Cassie to give me the rest of the tour including those other floors and answer some questions. Like, how had they managed to get the smell of smoke out of those books? And what precautions had they taken to make sure they didn't become the next Wheeler Field?

If they hadn't already. There were tons of stories on the news about flooded basements and ruined merchandise, including one about a designer shoe store's basement full of floating Ferragamos and Jimmy Choos.

There wasn't anything about Ozymandias Books, but the shoe store was on 48th. They could very well be in the same block. Which reminded me, I needed to find out the bookshop's address. Between the rain and talking to the cabbie and checking the time, I had no idea what street it was on.

I typed the name into my GPS app, hoping I wouldn't need an address for it, but it didn't work, and trying the same thing on MapQuest and Google Maps didn't either. And all googling "Ozymandias Books" brought up was a headshop in Boulder, Colorado, and Percy Bysshe Shelley's poem about a traveler in the desert who stumbles onto a monument to some forgotten pharaoh that has an inscription that says, "Look on my works, ye mighty, and despair," even though whatever "works" he'd had have long since disappeared.

Just like Ozymandias Books seemed to have done. I changed the search to "Ozymandias Bookstore."

That got me a bunch of bookstores which had copies of *Ozymandias and Other Poems* and *Shelley's Complete Works* for sale and a coffee-shop/used books-and-records/internet café in Dubuque. I refined the search to "Ozymandias Bookstore Manhattan."

That kicked up two bookstores in Manhattan, Kansas, and a book about the Manhattan Project. I changed Manhattan to NYC and got a list of thirty bookstores, including five Barnes and Nobles and the just-closed Elliott's, but not Ozymandias Books.

Come on, the address had to be listed somewhere. I didn't have time to walk all over Manhattan looking for it. I googled "NYC bookshops," "NYC used books," and "NYC used bookstores" and then remembered Cassie's saying "We're not a bookstore," and tried "book preserve" and, even though she'd said it wasn't a library, "NY libraries."

That brought up a photo of the 1911 Albany Capitol fire, which made me wonder all over again how they'd gotten the books out—flames shot from every window in the old Victorian building.

There was no listing for Ozymandias's under "archive" either, and I eventually gave up and went to bed.

In the morning I tried "book storage" and "book depository" (which brought up the Kennedy assassination), and "rare books," with no results, and then had an idea. Maybe there was a phone book in my room, even though it was one of the things I'd posted about as going the way of the dodo, and I could find Ozymandias in it.

There wasn't, and the person at the desk downstairs didn't even know what a phone book was. "There's an Apple store in Times Square," she suggested tentatively. "They might have a book on phones, I guess."

I tried to explain what a phone book was and why I needed it.

"Can't you just look up the address on your phone?" she said.

'Why didn't I think of that?" I said, and since it looked like the rain had more or less stopped, went out to see if I could find the place on foot.

I had a general idea of the bookshop's location— somewhere in the upper Forties or low Fifties between Madison Avenue and Broadway, which was only an area of twenty blocks, and I could eliminate some of them right off the bat. Obviously Ozymandias's hadn't been on the same block as Grand Central Station or 30 Rock, or I'd have noticed.

And I'd be able to eliminate others by what I remembered of the street Ozymandias's was on. It had been in the middle of the block, in a recessed doorway, and there'd been a deli in the same block and a souvenir shop—and maybe a florist's? or a nail salon? and somewhere in there some hoardings where they were repairing one of the buildings, all of which should make my job easier.

That's what I thought. It only took me half an hour to realize what I told you at the beginning, that *all* of Manhattan's streets have delis and scaffolding and souvenir shops and that all of them look exactly alike.

The taxi driver who'd taken me to Random House. He might remember where he'd picked me up. But I had no idea what the taxi's number was, and I'd paid cash and jumped out the minute we got there, so I didn't have a receipt either, and I only vaguely remembered what the driver had looked like. He'd had an accent, but I had a feeling that in New York wasn't going to be enough to narrow it down.

I *did* remember what the fare had been—six-eighty. I hailed a cab, got in, and asked the driver, "If the destination was Fifty-Seventh and Broadway, and the fare was six-eighty, how many blocks would you have taken me?"

He had an accent, too. "Are you saying I cheat my customers?" he said, and ordered me out.

"Wait," I said. "Do you know what street Ozymandias Books is on?"

"Out. Before I call 911."

I got out, and went back to walking the blocks again, going up and down them till they blurred into an endless stream of pizzerias and shoe repairs and Starbucks, and I had no idea which blocks I'd checked and which I hadn't. Or what damned street I was on.

It was like when I'd gotten lost in Ozymandias's stacks looking for the bookburning section, with no idea of how to get back to where I'd been or even where I was, and every aisle of books looking exactly like every other.

I went back to the souvenir shop I'd just passed, bought a tourist map and a pen shaped like the Empire State Building (the only kind they had) and tried again, this time crossing each block off on the map as I finished walking it, and marking each corner deli, each souvenir shop. I found lots of them and *lots* of scaffolding, but no Ozymandias Books.

Maybe it was in one of those blocks I'd previously eliminated. It had, after all, been raining, and I'd been focused on finding shelter, not on my surroundings. I walked up to Rockefeller Center, but one look at the skating rink and that giant gold statue of whatever it is convinced me I couldn't have *not* noticed it, even in a deluge.

That meant it wasn't in the blocks I'd mapped out and I must have walked farther north after that interview than I'd realized. I expanded the search up to Fifty-Third Street, which took me the rest of the day, and the next morning enlarged it farther, over to Park Avenue.

Still nothing. Could it have been farther south? I expanded the grid again, down to Thirty-Eighth Street and then Thirty-Fourth.

Maybe there'll be another miracle on Thirty-Fourth Street, I thought, *and Ozymandias's'll be there, right next door to Macy's.*

But the only thing next door to Macy's was a Victoria's Secret and then the Empire State Building, and when I stepped out into the street to try to see what was in the next block down from *that*, I was nearly hit by a cab.

That gave me an idea. Just because the taxi driver hadn't known where Ozymandias's Books was (or wouldn't tell me), it didn't mean somebody wouldn't. I went back up to Forty-Fifth and started walking the blocks I'd originally checked, this time stopping in every coffee shop and bar and barber shop I came to and asking them if they knew where

Ozymandias Books was and/or if they knew of a bookstore in this neighborhood.

I got answers ranging from "Never heard of it," to "There used to be a bookstore over on Eighth Avenue, but it closed last year," to "No bookstores in this part of town. The rents are too steep."

It was getting dark. I'd only covered about a third of the territory I'd mapped out to ask people in, but I was dog-tired. I took a taxi back to the hotel, watching the meter and trying to calculate the price per block, still hoping to locate Ozymandias's that way, but no dice—the fare was based on time, not distance, and when I got back to the hotel, I got a text from Brooke wanting me to call her. I hoped it didn't mean the Random House guy was coming back sooner than expected.

It didn't, but it was almost as bad. She'd set up a bunch of interviews and meetings for me for the next few days.

"No," I said. "You need to cancel them."

"They won't be like the WMNH interview, I promise."

"That's not it. It's that I don't have time. I'm too busy to do any interviews or meetings."

"Busy? Doing what?" she asked. "Are you okay?"

"I'm fine," I said, hung up, found a hotel on Forty-Eighth so I'd be closer to the search area (and so Brooke couldn't come over and drag me off to meetings), moved my stuff over to it, and got on Google Earth, wondering why I hadn't thought of that before.

It rapidly became apparent. Because it was designed for finding a particular address and zeroing in on it, not scanning whole streets, and the resolution wasn't good enough to always make out the numbers above the doors, particularly on the office buildings.

Office buildings. Maybe that's what I should be looking for, since I was having so much trouble finding the bookstore. When I'd come up, it had been into an old-fashioned office-building lobby with a revolving door. If I could find *it*, I could simply take the elevator down to the stacks. Plus, it had to have been only a few doors down, a block at the most, from the bookshop entrance. Using it as a point to orient myself by, I could find Ozymandias's itself.

Except I couldn't find the damned lobby either. I spent I don't know how many days looking for it with no luck. It wasn't that there weren't any revolving doors or lobbies. There were scores of them, a lot with the marble walls and old-fashioned brass grillwork I remembered, but not the one I'd raced through to get to my taxi.

I tried their elevators anyway, but they only went down one or two levels and opened onto cobwebby furnaces or suspicious building supers. Or both.

You're going to have to try something else, I told myself when I got back to my hotel after a particularly frustrating day. But what? I supposed I could ask Brooke if *she* knew where Ozymandias Books was. She was a native New Yorker. But if I called her, she'd demand to know why I'd been ignoring all her messages and texts, and I was afraid she'd start talking about meetings and interviews again, and I didn't have time for that.

And if I called the WMNH interview guy, he'd go off on a rant about the death of the independent bookstore.

I was on my own here. I supposed in the morning I could expand the search area again—or the kinds of lobbies to look at. I'd been in a tearing hurry to get to my appointment that night and hadn't really gotten a good look at the lobby—or the door. Maybe I'd been wrong about it having been a revolving door.

But I couldn't do either of those till morning. Till then, I decided to call up that list of New York City bookstores I'd found earlier and ask the ones that were still open if *they'd* heard of Ozymandias Books. I figured if anybody'd be likely to know where it was, they would.

But they didn't, and, halfway through the list, I realized I was going about this all wrong. The *books* were the way to find it. If the ones on Ozymandias's shelves really were among the last copies in the world, then googling their titles would lead me there, as the only place they could be found. I typed in *Ambush in Apache Canyon.*

Three items came up—a Wikipedia entry that turned out to be one of those space holders for an unwritten entry, a blog post by someone else who'd read the book when he was a kid and wanted to buy a copy, which ended, "If anybody knows where I can purchase one, I'd be willing to pay top dollar. I can't find one anywhere!" and a listing on Amazon.

I'd thought Cassie had said they weren't a bookstore, and this might be some other copy and she was exaggerating how rare their books were, but it was worth a try. I clicked on it.

But all it showed under "Copies Available" was a dash, which meant they didn't actually have the book, and when I tried AbeBooks, it said, "No exact match. Do you care to expand your search?"

No, that was the last thing I wanted. The whole point was to narrow it down, not make it broader. I tried looking for the book on BookFinder and Alibris.

It wasn't listed on any of them.

But Cassie had said it had just come in recently. Maybe they hadn't had time to list it. I needed to try some other title. If I could remember one. There'd been a *Vagabond Boys Going Somewhere Or Other*, but I had no idea where, and a *Grace Harlowe at Some College or Other*. And *The Dionne Quintuplets in Hollywood*. I tried that.

Nothing. "No longer in print," the online bookstores read, and "Unavailable," and when I checked

Project Gutenberg and Google Books, it wasn't there either.

Why not? If Ozymandias was an archive like Cassie said, why hadn't the books they had been digitized? What good was it to save all those books if you weren't going to make them available to scholars?

Maybe it was just that scholars weren't interested in preserving *The Dionne Quintuplets* or *Ambush in Apache Canyon*. I needed to come up with a more important book—or author.

There'd been a Shakespeare—what was its name?— and a Poe and a Melville, but I needed exact titles.

I stared at the laptop screen, trying to remember the books in those first shelves by the baggage chute. But Cassie'd said those hadn't been catalogued yet, so they probably wouldn't have made it online either, and neither would the ones in the bookshop. Or on the stairs. It was going to have to be something in the Floods section. Or in War.

Eventually, after several hours of trying to remember, I managed to come up with half a dozen titles: *Marooned on Saturn*, *New Theories of the Atom*, *Visitations from Beyond the Veil*, *Tommy Toad's Birthday Surprise*, *Dirigibles: Our Future*, and *Noah's Ark on Ararat*, the one that had been rescued from the Yancey Creek Carnegie Library flood.

But I didn't have any luck with them either, and when I googled *Following in the Master's Footsteps*, it didn't bring up anything at all, not even a dash on Amazon.

Jesus, the WMNH interview guy was right, I thought. *Things* do *disappear into the ether.*

I needed the name of a book that would be listed more than one place, one whose endangered state would cause an outcry, and not *The Vagabond Boys in Bryce Canyon*, whose name I'd just remembered. Its demise would hardly have been seen as a literary crisis.

What about those books Ozymandias's had rescued from the Great Fire of London? What had been their names? It didn't matter. I could google "St. Paul's fire books," and find them that way.

I did. It brought up a bunch of articles about the London Blitz and a bookstore fire in St. Paul, Minnesota. I googled "St. Paul's fire 1667 books" instead. And stared at the screen.

"Thousands of books had been stored for safekeeping in St. Paul's," the screen read. "Attempts were made to direct the fire away from it, but they proved useless. The roof caught fire, and within hours the church lay in ashes."

"That's not true," I said to my laptop. "St. Paul's didn't burn down. It's still there. They must be talking about some other church," and looked up, "History of St. Paul's *Cathedral*."

I'd been right. St. Paul's, with its famous dome, hadn't burned down. But this wasn't that St. Paul's. It was its predecessor, the thirteenth century wood-and-stone cathedral Christopher Wren had been hired to rebuild. After the Great Fire of London burned the first one down.

"As the flames approached, booksellers and publishers from the surrounding streets had stored their inventories in St. Paul's in an attempt to keep them safe," the screen read, "but the effort proved fruitless as their books perished along with the cathedral."

They didn't all perish, I thought, *At least a few of them survived*, and clicked on *London: A Compleat History* to see if it listed the titles. "The books had been stored in the safest area possible, the crypt," it said, "but as the fire progressed, the lead of the roof melted and ran down between the cathedral's building stones, and the roof itself collapsed through the crypt's roof."

Just like Wheeler Field," I murmured, and clicked on Moseby's *A Full History of the Great Fire*.

It read, "Tens of thousands of books were destroyed, including Sir William Dugdale's *Originales Judiciales*, *The History of Embanking and Draining*, Sir Thomas Urquhart's *The Jewel*, and every copy of the just-published *The Carolies* by John Ogilbie."

"Not every one," I said.

I read on. "The air in the crypt had been superheated by the surrounding flames, and when the roof collapsed, it ignited in a fireball that instantly incinerated all the volumes stored there for safekeeping."

"Then how did they get that copy of *The Carolies* out?" I said.

They didn't, I thought, a sick feeling settling in my gut. That's why Cassie wasn't worried about flooding. And why she'd given me that pitying look when I'd said I'd have to find my copy of *Ambush in Apache Canyon* and read it again.

But that's impossible. They have to have saved it, I thought, and googled "Lewis Carroll's diaries."

A whole page of sites came up, and I felt a rush of relief. "There, you see?" I said, and clicked on the first one. "Charles Dodgson's personal diaries, kept by him from 1855 on," it read. "Only Volumes 2, 4, 5, and 8–12 remain in existence. Volumes 1, 3, 6, and 7 and several additional pages were burned by his family after his death."

The sick feeling was back. I hastily called up the next site. "Lost Literary Treasures," it was headed, and under that it said, "The following books and manuscripts are known to have been written, but no longer exist." It listed *Richard Crookback* and *Cardenio* and Gibbon's *History of the Liberty of the Swiss*.

"No," I said, and googled Sylvia Plath and scrolled through her bibliography, looking for the title I'd seen.

Double Exposure. That was it. Or *Double Take.* Nobody knew for sure—because it had been destroyed, too, either by Sylvia or her husband. They weren't sure about that.

But they were sure it was gone. "No copy of the book is known to remain in existence."

No.

I googled the Yancey Creek Library Flood. "Due to the swiftness of the rising waters," the local newspaper account said, "librarians were unable to save any of the library's contents, including the library's extensive, irreplaceable genealogical records."

They couldn't save Noah's Ark on Ararat *either,* I thought, looking at the photo that accompanied the article. It showed the building completely submerged, only the roof and the word "Carnegie" showing above water.

Below it was a second picture, taken a week later, of a front loader dredging up a scoopful of disgusting-looking muck which had once been books and was now a muddy, foul-smelling glop, and preparing to dump it in a giant trash bin.

Because there was no way to salvage those books. Just like there was no way to restore the moldy, rat-feces-covered volumes in those hoarders' houses or put back together the ones blown up by bombs or burned to ashes.

And that was why there hadn't been any smell of smoke in the Fires section, and no sprinkler system, no listings on AbeBooks or BookFinder or Alibris. There weren't any books to list.

It explained everything—why Melville's *The Isle of the Cross* was there and not *Moby Dick*—which there were tons of copies of—why Cassie hated libraries so much, why so many of the books were old. Cassie was right. Time was the biggest enemy of books. Over the years, copy after copy would fall prey to wars and weather, to bookworms and bookburnings and fraying bindings, disintegrating paper, careless children, till at last there was only one left in some college library or old lady's attic, and when she died or the library needed to make room for more banks of computers, it succumbed, too. And came tumbling down the baggage chute into Ozymandias's.

Ozymandias's wasn't a book preserve—it was a morgue, and the books were shelved not by the disaster they'd been rescued from but by what had done them in. And the reason I couldn't find it was because it wasn't there either.

But it has to be. I was there. I was on those stairs, in those stacks. I *saw* Cassie take out those books and look at them.

Which means they—and Ozymandias's—are here somewhere, and the reason I haven't been able to find it is because the entrance is somehow hidden.

After the flooding, a lot of storefronts were screened off by plastic sheeting and equipment pumping out the water, or the door might be blocked by hoardings or scaffolding or a parked delivery truck.

Or I somehow skipped the block when I was searching. Like I told you, all the streets look exactly the same, and now there are Christmas lights and snowflakes and Santas in all the windows, making them look even more alike.

Or maybe I've been looking in the wrong part of Manhattan. It occurred to me yesterday that that first day, when it started to rain and I was focused on finding shelter and/or an umbrella, I might somehow have gotten turned around without realizing it and headed back south—or east—and I should be looking over on Lexington Avenue or down in the Twenties. And checking out the subway stations.

When Jude called in that day, she said the station was flooded and she was going to have to find a taxi, so that means she usually comes to work by subway, and if I wait at the station entrance, at the top of the stairs, I might be able to spot her and get her to take me there so Cassie can explain everything, can tell me how *The Carolies* was miraculously saved from the Great Fire, how Ogilbie's publisher snatched it up as he fled, and how *Noah's Ark on Ararat* had been checked out when the flood hit the Yancey Creek Public Library and a robot submersible brought up *The Plight of the Vicar's Daughter* and *A Brief History of Ocean Travel* from the *Titanic*. And my copy of *Ambush in Apache Canyon* is safely in my mother's basement—even though when I called her she said she'd donated all my old books to her church rummage sale after I graduated.

Cassie can tell me she's wrong, that *Ambush in Apache Canyon* wasn't sent to the sale, that she missed it because it was hidden in among a bunch of old videotapes and thirty-five-millimeter slides. Just like Ozymandias's is hidden in among the cleaners and pizzerias and souvenir shops. All I have to do is find the subway station and Jude. Or that lobby where I came up. Or the recessed doorway of the bookshop itself.

I know it's here someplace. Because if it isn't, all those books I saw (and who knows how many since then? I just read on my phone about a famous bookstore in Seattle closing) have vanished.

And everything I said about our only allowing things we don't need to disappear was a gigantic lie. There's no decision-making in the process. It's all completely accidental—a conflagration here, a teething puppy there, leaky pipes and wars and peanut butter and bookworms and bookburnings and book-culling and being left out in the rain.

Aided by our well-meaning attempts to stop the slaughter by microfilming them and digitizing them and parking them all together in the middle of the field. And assuming there are plenty of copies around, and that sending one more to the landfill won't matter. Till all that's left is a dash on Amazon and sometimes not even that.

And we don't even know they're gone. At least when the Library of Alexandria burned, we knew it. Here, it's happening in front of our very eyes, and we can't even see it. Till we try to find a copy of a book we loved as a kid. Or accidentally stumble into Ozymandias's.

Brooke just called again, demanding to know why I hadn't shown up to my meeting with Random House. "This is the fifth time I've rescheduled it," she said. "I can't keep covering for you like this. What's your excuse this time? And don't tell me research. What are you really doing? I called your hotel and they told me you'd checked out three weeks ago. Have you gotten involved with someone?"

Yes, I thought, scanning the faces coming along the street for Jude's, for Cassie's.

"You can do whatever you want with your love life, but this is your career we're talking about. And mine. And you're destroying both of them," Brooke said, but she sounded more concerned than angry. "Are you okay?" she asked. "What's going on?"

They're gone, I thought. *All those books.* Double Exposure *and* Ambush in Apache Canyon, *Raleigh and Lewis Carroll and* Tommy Toad *and* The Daring

Debutante, *and thousands, millions of others. And more of them disappear every day, tumbling down that chute from fires and hoarders' houses and book sales, so fast that even working extra hours and calling in Jude and Thaddeus and Rita and everybody else Cassie can think of to help, there's no way they'll be able to keep up with the deluge.*

"I said, are you okay?" Brooke repeated. "I'm worried about you. Have you gotten in some kind of trouble? Where are you?"

"I don't know," I said, looking vaguely around at the delis and hoardings and souvenir shops surrounding me. "All the streets look alike."

There was a silence, and then she said, sounding very calm, "Listen, I want you to find a taxi and tell them to take you to my office. I'll pay for it. I'll be waiting for you outside on the sidewalk, and we'll work this all out, whatever it is. Just find a taxi and come here to me. Okay?"

"Yes," I said, but I can't. I have to find Ozymandias's first. It's here someplace, on one of these endless, look-alike streets. It has to be.

Because otherwise all those endless shelves of books—all those histories and plays and adventures and sentimental novels and textbooks and teen star biographies are gone. And whatever fascinating or affecting or profound things that were in them are as lost to us as that vanished kingdom of

Ozymandias's. Look on my works, ye mighty, and despair indeed.

And I know, I know, most of them were junk, and nobody's going to miss *The Vagabond Boys* or *Chickens is Chickens*. But what about *Cardenio* and Edgar Allan Poe's story and *The Carolies* and *Ambush in Apache Canyon*? And even *The Dionne Quintuplets in Hollywood* might have had something important to say to us.

But now we'll never know. Because, in spite of what I told the interview guy on WMNH, in spite of what I believed, there isn't any way to get them back. They are, as I so carelessly, so callously, put it, gone for good. And we let them go.

But that's too terrible a thought to even contemplate. We can't just have let them all disappear without a trace like that, can we?

Surely not. Which means there's some other explanation for all this, and the books are just endangered and there's still time to save them. I just have to find Ozymandias. It's here somewhere, on one of these goddamn look-alike streets. It has to be.